WO! NEMO, TOSS A LASSO TO ME NOW!

(AND OTHER PALINDROMES)

by Dona Smith

Illustrated by Kimble Mead

D0030490

SCHOLASTIC INC.

New York Toronto London Auckland Sydney

For Chris, Emma, and Perry

ISBN 0-590-47710-2

Copyright © 1993 by Scholastic Inc.
All rights reserved. Published by Scholastic Inc.

12 11 10 9 8 7 6 5 4 3 2 1   3 4 5 6 7 8 9 / 9

Printed in the U.S.A   01

First Scholastic printing, December 1993

What's a Palindrome?

A palindrome is a word, phrase, or sentence that reads the same backward and forward. The words DID, POP, and BIB, for example, are palindromes. WO! NEMO, TOSS A LASSO TO ME NOW! is a longer palindrome. There are even *famous* palindromes, such as A MAN, A PLAN, A CANAL, PANAMA, and ENID AND EDNA DINE.

New palindromes are being invented every day. How would you go about creating your own? Well, it's generally agreed that the best way is to start with the word in the middle and build your way outward. I found that this worked for me, while starting at one end seemed like a bad idea.

A palindrome doesn't have to be complicated — straw warts, for example, is a fine palindrome. A palindrome can be silly — in fact, sometimes, the sillier the better. But it should make *some* kind of sense. We can't have much fun with GOT PAN A NAP TOG.

Finally, palindromes lend themselves to some *really looney* illustrations. Start turning the pages and take a look!

Dona Smith

OTTO
SEES
OTTO

MARGE
LETS NORAH
SEE SHARON'S
TELEGRAM

MADAM, I'M ADAM

TACO
CAT

NEVER
EVER
EVEN

A DIET:
A SALAD,
ALAS,
ATE IDA

STAR
RATS

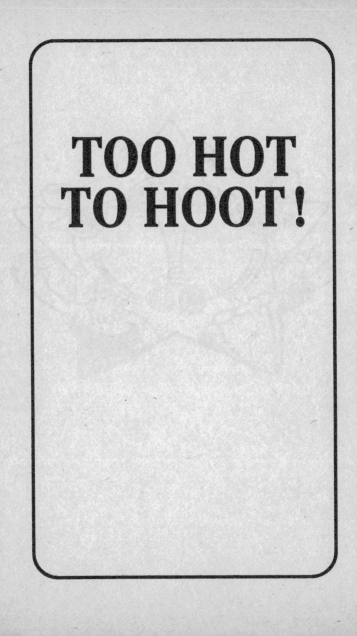

TOO HOT
TO HOOT!

WO! NEMO, TOSS A LASSO TO ME NOW!

ENID
AND EDNA
DINE

A MAN,
A PLAN,
A CANAL,
PANAMA

DUDE
DUD

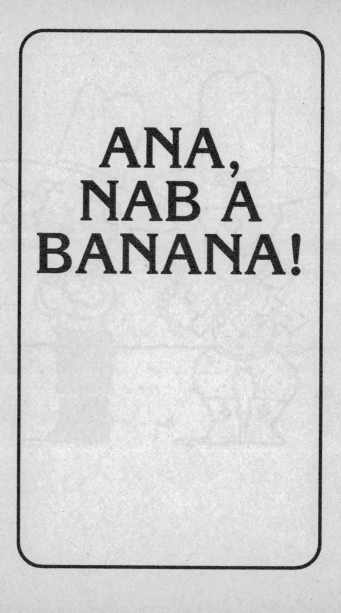

ANA,
NAB A
BANANA!

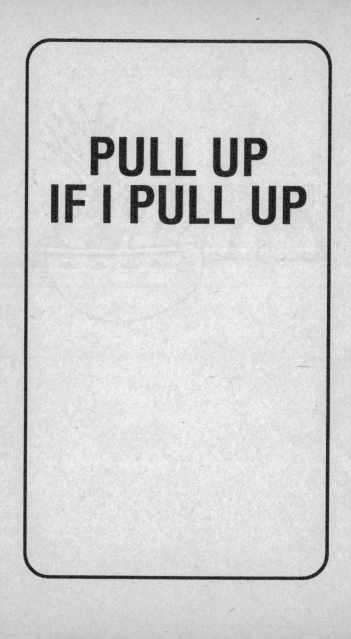

PULL UP
IF I PULL UP

TANGO
GNAT

ABLE WAS I,
'ERE I SAW ELBA

I MIME
MIMI

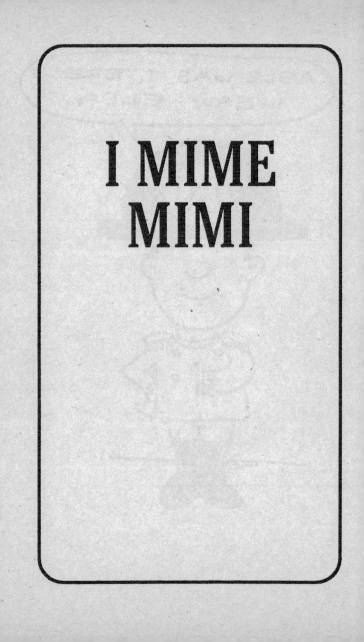

WON TON?
NOT NOW!

SPACE
CAPS

PETS TELL ABE BALLET STEP

RATS
AT A BAR
GRAB AT A
STAR

TENT
NET

WAS
IT A CAR
OR A
CAT I SAW?

REWARD
DRAWER

MEGA
GEM

TUNA ROLL, OR A NUT?

STUNT
NUTS

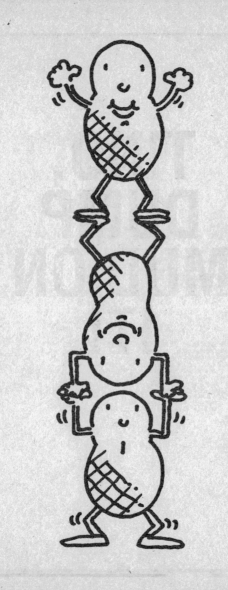

TINO,
DUMP
MUD ON
IT!

NOEL,
LEON!

POOR DAN
IS IN
A DROOP

BANK
NAB

SMART
RAMS

WAS IT ELIOT'S TOILET I SAW?

NOLA'S
SALON

NIAGARA, O ROAR AGAIN!

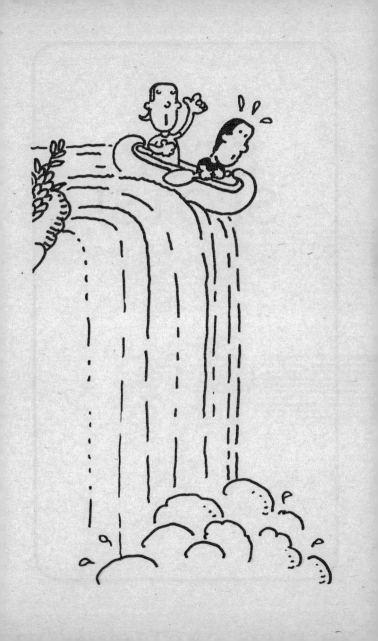

STOP,
SPOTS!

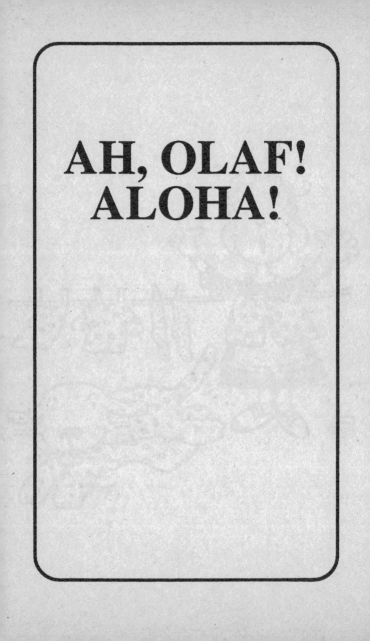

AH, OLAF!
ALOHA!

YELL
ALLEY

TEN ANIMALS I SLAM IN A NET

DIARY
RAID

WE SEW,
EWE SEW

KAYAK
A YAK

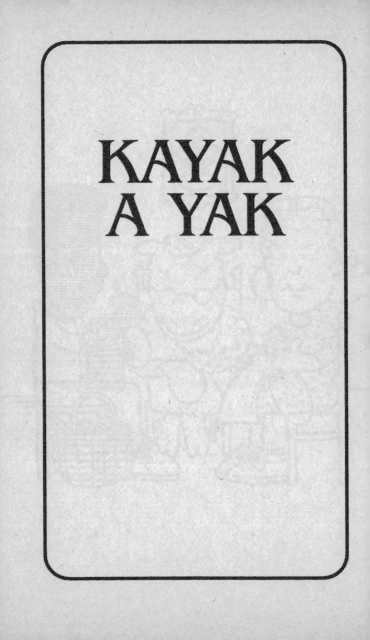

MY
GYM

SOME MEN INTERPRET NINE MEMOS

WORM
ROW

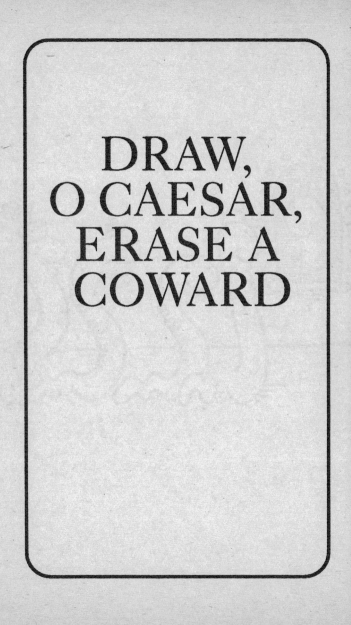

DRAW,
O CAESAR,
ERASE A
COWARD